First published by Parragon in 2013
Parragon
Chartist House
15–17 Trim Street
Bath BA1 1HA, UK
www.parragon.com

Written by Peter Bently
Illustrated by Emma Foster and Deborah Melmon
Edited by Laura Baker
Designed by Rachael Fisher and Jo Russell
Production by Jonathan Wakeham
All photos courtesy of iStockphoto

ISBN 978-1-4723-0290-8

Printed in China

Bunny Loves to Write

PaRRagon

Bath · New York · Singapore · Hong Kong · Cologne · Delhi
Melbourne · Amsterdam · Johannesburg · Shenzhen

One day, Buster was going out to play.
"Always carrying a book!" chuckled Mum. "What is it this time, Buster? An adventure? A ghost story?"

"It's not a storybook," smiled Buster. "It's a notebook.
My teacher wants everyone in the class to make up a story."
"That sounds fun," said Mum. "What will you write?"

"I don't know," said Buster.
"I can't think of anything!"
"Oh, you'll soon have lots of
ideas," said Mum. "But write
them down at once or you'll
forget them!"

Buster started walking to the park. He soon met his friend Francine.

"Mum packed us a picnic," she said. "Lend me a paw with this heavy basket!"

"A picnic? It feels more like treasure!" grunted Buster.

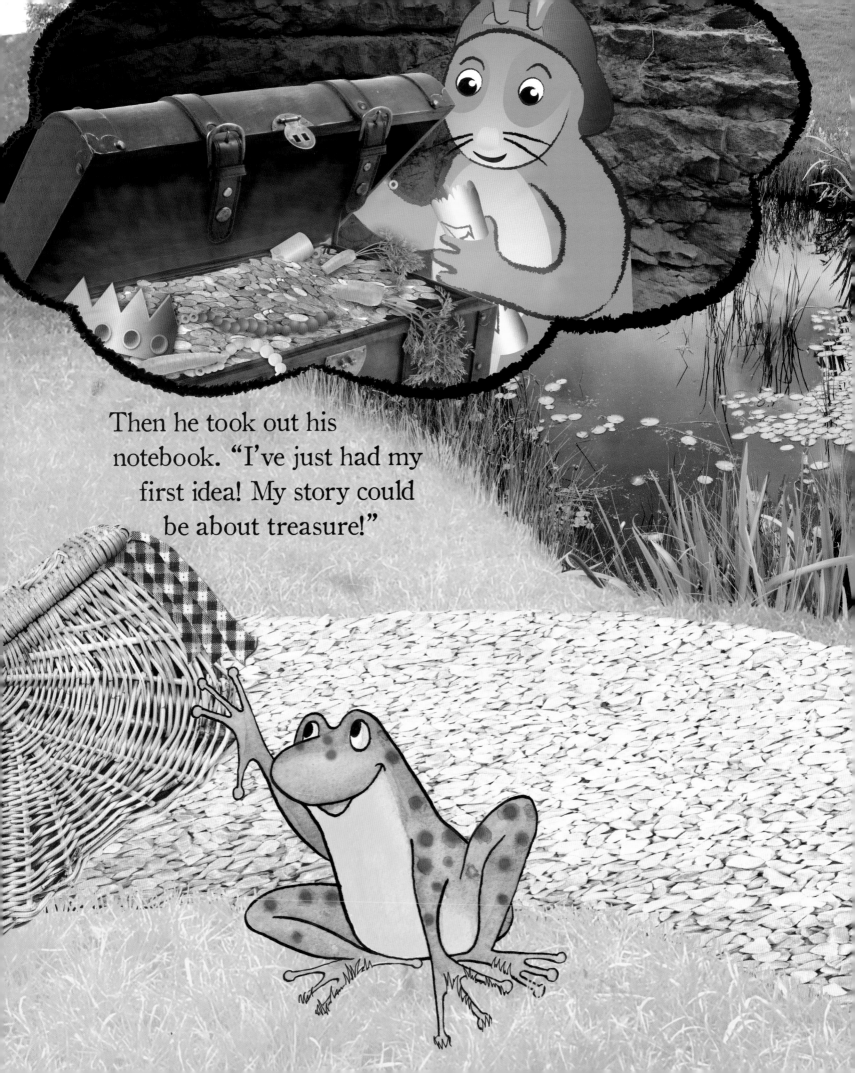

Then he took out his notebook. "I've just had my first idea! My story could be about treasure!"

They carried on towards the park,
but soon Francine stopped.
"I'm sure I just saw Max," she said.

"Me too," puzzled Buster. "But he seems
to have disappeared!"
"As if by magic!" smiled Francine.

"Magic, eh?" said Buster. "Maybe someone could do magic in my story. Like a wizard!"

Suddenly…

BOO!

Max jumped out from behind a bush.
"Eek! You gave me a fright!" laughed Francine.

"And you've given me another idea," said Buster. "Something scary! There could be spooky ghosts in my story!"

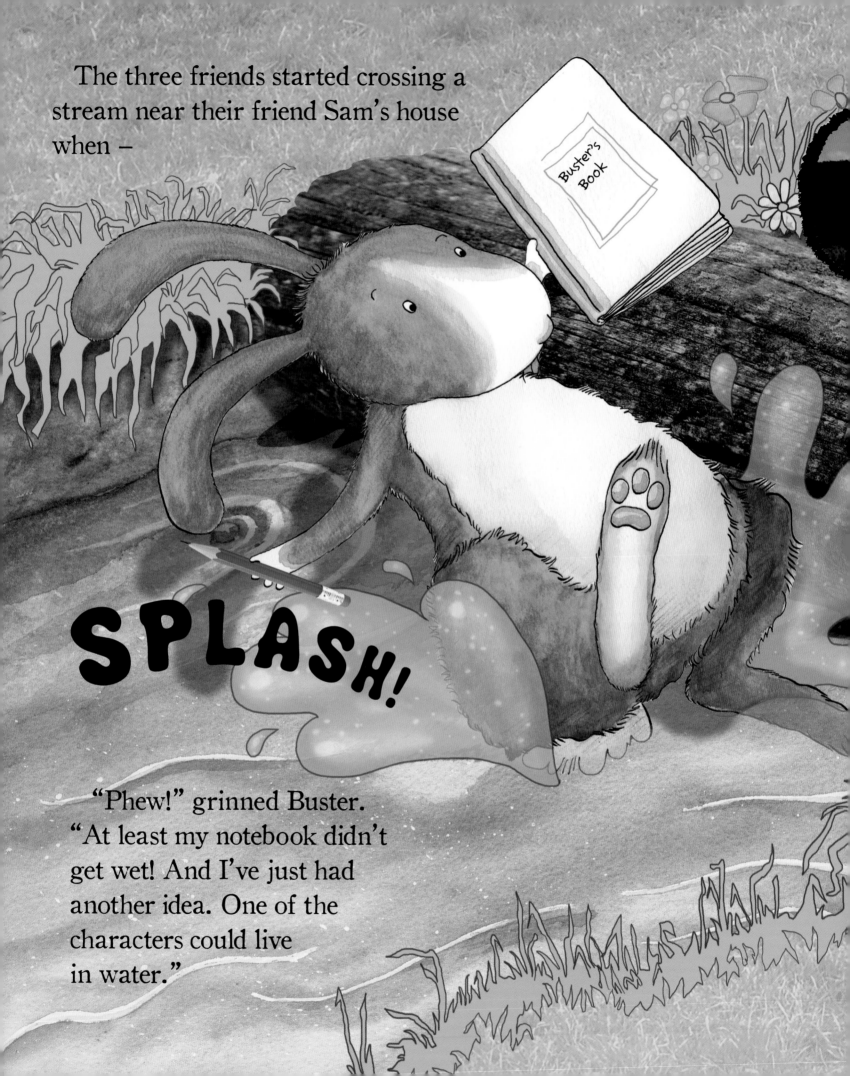

The three friends started crossing a stream near their friend Sam's house when —

SPLASH!

"Phew!" grinned Buster. "At least my notebook didn't get wet! And I've just had another idea. One of the characters could live in water."

"Like a mermaid," suggested Max.
"Or a frog!" said Francine.

"Hi, everyone," said Sam.
"I'll be ready in a minute.
Do you want to come up and
wait?"

Sam's
Place

"What, up there?" gasped Francine.
"No way! You're almost in the sky!"

"Now there's an idea," said Buster. "There could be planes in my story."

"Or space rockets," said Max. "Or aliens!" said Francine.

When they got to the park, the friends met Bella, Buster's sister.

"Hi, everyone!" she said. "Hey, Buster, what are you writing?"

"I'm writing a story," said Buster. "I've had lots of ideas and now I'm making them into a proper adventure!"

"Cool," said Bella.
"Can we hear it?"
"Okay..." said Buster.
"But it isn't finished yet."
Buster opened his notebook and began to read.

One day Gus and Ella found a chest in the attic. It was so heavy!

Like my picnic basket!

They opened the lid.
The chest was
full of gold!

"Thank you!" said the wizard.
"You found the lost
treasure of Meowlin!"

But the very next night,
the treasure vanished.

Where had it gone?

So the wizard waved his wand and they all flew to Mars by magic!

"That's as far as I got," sighed Buster. "I told you it wasn't finished."

"We'll finish it for you!" cried Sam.

"Cool!" said Buster. "You can all write a bit each."

Everyone took it in turns writing in
Buster's notebook.
"Okay," he said when they had finished.
"Here's the rest of the story!"

The wizard tricked the aliens and took back the chest.

That's my bit!

Brilliant, thanks, everyone! There's just one last thing to add.

And he wrote:

Gus, Ella, Freya and the wizard all lived happily ever after.

THE END

"Hooray!" said Francine. "But the story isn't quite finished."

"Isn't it?" said Buster. "What happens next?"

"Easy," laughed Francine. "They all eat the treasure!"